Stone Underpants

This book belongs to:

Amber ♡

Stone Underpants
is an original concept by
© 2018 Rebecca Lisle

Author: Rebecca Lisle
Illustrator: Richard Watson

First Published in the UK in 2016 by **MAVERICK ARTS PUBLISHING LTD**

Studio 3A, City Business Centre, 6 Brighton Road,
Horsham, West Sussex, RH13 5BB
© Maverick Arts Publishing Limited 2016
+44 (0)1403 256941

American edition published in 2018 by Maverick Arts Publishing, distributed
in the United States and Canada by Lerner Publishing Group Inc., 241 First
Avenue North, Minneapolis, MN 55401 USA

distributed by **Lerner**

ISBN 978-1-84886-311-8

Stone Underpants

by Rebecca Lisle

illustrated by
Richard Watson

It was cold in the Stone Age.
When the icy wind blew it was freezing.

"I really do need something to keep my bottom warm," Pod told his Dad.
"You could make something," Dad said.
"Stone is very handy."

Pod **smashed** and **chiseled**.

He **chipped** and **sanded**.

Pod made himself some
super stone underpants.

"Yahoo! These are great!"
He put them on and went out to play.

His friends were angry.
"Oh Pod! Now they've scored a goal!"

"Yahoo! GOAL!"

the other team shouted.

Pod and his friends went to the lake. They all jumped in. His friends **bobbed** back up.

But Pod sank down.

Pod threw his underpants away.
"So much for the Stone Age!"

Pod tried again, this time with **WOOD**.

Pod **cut** and he **sawed**.

He **hammered** and he **nailed**.

And he made himself a pair of **wooden underpants**. They were light and airy. But they were very scratchy and...

...SPLINTERY!

"OW!"

In the night Pod's wooden underpants mysteriously disappeared.

"Stone's no good. Wood's no use. But I still need some bottom warmers!" What could he use now?

Shells were too **clattery**.

Spider webs were too **sticky**.

Mud was too **yucky**.

Pod searched for feathers.
Not every bird wanted to share.

At last Pod had enough feathers.

He **wove** and he **cut**. He **plaited** and he **sewed**.

The fluffy
feather underpants
were light and soft and
deliciously warm.

When he played soccer he could...run

...jump

...and kick.

But...

He **twitched** and **twisted**.
He **squirmed** and **wriggled**.
The feathers tickled him so much he missed
the ball and bounced headfirst into a swamp.

The feather underpants
were too **ticklish** for Pod...

But his mom really liked them.

What a lovely feather duster!

Pod's bottom was
still cold, but...

Hoosh Hoosh

"Hello warm, woolly mammoth," said Pod.
"Ooo! Your coat's given me a great idea!"

Pod's needles **clicked** and **clacked**.
He **knitted** and **knotted**.

Pod loved his new **woolly underpants**.

Now climbing trees was **easy**.

Kicking balls was **great**.

Swimming was **super**.

And best of all...

"My bottom is so
TOASTY!"

The End

I think I've invented the bronze age!